Matt Shaw Publications

www.mattshawpublications.co.uk

www.facebook.com/mattshawpublications

Twisted Bitches

MATT SHAW and MICHAEL BRAY

#1

NOW

The Club.

Dance music pumped into the two-storey nightclub; a square building with a dance-floor on the ground level with a bar on two sides. The second floor was more of a viewing gallery than anything else: a large bar for people to get drinks, seating areas made up of small tables and large, comfortable sofas of a deep red colour and a cut away in the centre of the room - surrounded by a wall – where you could look down to the dancers below. Couples danced with the majority of the men behind their partners, the girls backed up against them, grinding hard. Dirty dancing. Other couples faced each other, lust in their eyes as they too bumped against each other provocatively. Sweat dripping off them as the bright flashing lights hanging overhead shone down on them, just them. Some couples had arrived together, some were meeting for the first time and would soon part ways and others - meeting for the first time - would be leaving together to continue the fun elsewhere. A typical Saturday night then; the kind of night *she* hated.

Harley was on the second-floor of the club. She was leaning over the balcony in a low-top contour dress that stopped just above the knees. No panties so no visible panty-line. Her breasts were pushed together by both dress and bra. Harley hated these places. To her, they were nothing but a cattle market for the horny men and yet here she was, dressed to impress, giving them exactly what they looked for; a sexy view.

Half past midnight and she had seen many people get together with the men mainly responsible for the initial chat-up. She couldn't hear what was said but presumed it was the usual. Cheesy chat-up lines which shouldn't work and yet, when enough alcohol is consumed, somehow do.

'I may not be Fred Flintstone but I can make your bed rock.'

'Can I have your picture so I can show Santa what I want for Christmas?'

'Guess what I am wearing... The smile you gave me.'

'Your hand looks heavy, can I hold it for you?'

'Do you have a name or can I call you "mine"?'

As Harley imagined the lines, she tried not to show disgust on her face or throw up in her mouth. Neither action would attract a member of the opposite sex...

Not everyone was paired up. Those who hadn't were standing in a similar position to Harley, leaning over the balcony looking down at their potential targets. As Harley scanned the various faces around the balcony, she couldn't help but laugh at the men's stupidity. They want to *cop off* with a girl for the night, maybe even take them back to their place, and yet they were looking down at people who had already paired up. Sure, there were groups of girls dancing together down there too - friends on a night out - but surely the men couldn't be so stupid as to think they would be approachable? Girls dancing together were not good targets to approach if you were looking to *pull.* They were with their friends, out having fun, and the last thing they wanted was a man trying to separate them. No. If the men wanted to pull, they should spend more time looking around at the girls standing by themselves watching other people dancing with - what Harley hoped to be - an envious look on their faces. *Did she look envious, or were her true feelings on show?* She had been in the club for well over an hour now and it wasn't usually this long before someone made an approach. Harley shivered at the thought when - out of the corner of her eye - she noticed someone come and stand to the side of her. A man. Through her peripheral vision, she could tell he was looking directly at her. She turned to him with the best "neutral" expression she could muster.

'Hi,' he shouted over the music. 'Without trying to sound like a creep, I've been watching you and noticed three things.'

'Oh?'

'The first was that you're beautiful...'

Don't throw up.

'Thank you,' she said, smiling coyly; a smile well practised in front of the bathroom mirror in her sister's flat.

'The second was that you're all alone.' He paused a moment waiting for her to correct him. Perhaps she had a boyfriend with her and he had gone to the bathroom or was in one of the long queues at the bar? When she didn't respond, he continued, 'And the third was that you didn't have a drink.' Harley both loved and hated this part of the evening. On the one hand, if she played her cards right, she could leave the shit-hole club soon enough and get away from the stink of desperation and testosterone. On the other hand having to play *nice* while the men made their awkward moves was just painful. *Means to an end.* 'May I get you a drink?' he asked, cutting straight to the chase.

'I'll have a vodka and orange.'

The man smiled. To be fair, he wasn't bad looking. Not perfect by any stretch of the imagination but not the worst she had seen, or gone home with. Dark hair, slicked back, and green eyes. Light stubble from a few days growth. He wore black trousers with black, polished shoes and a white shirt which looked to be designer in make. Harley had definitely been with worse...

#2

BEFORE

The Room.

The girl opened her eyes, wincing at the steady rhythmic drum of a headache. She was on her back staring up at a yellowed ceiling she didn't recognise, tracing the innocuous dark damp stain with her eyes, a map drawn in disrepair in a room she was unfamiliar with. She waded through the soup that had replaced her mind and in doing so had discarded all rational thought and memory. Recollection was as unfamiliar as the room, and so, for now, she would have to focus on what she knew. This situation wasn't unfamiliar to her. Waking up in a strange house after a drink fuelled one night stand was standard practice, one that no matter how many times she regretted it would not shake itself. She didn't remember going out, and wasn't entirely sure the headache that pulsed and thrummed with anger behind her eyes was even a hangover, but either way, she knew she had made another mistake, another regret to add to the list that was rapidly growing too long to remember. She breathed in and wrinkled her nose. The musty scent of damp burned her sinuses, and she let out a short bark of a cough. The girl sat up, tired springs on the iron bedstead creaking in protest. She threw off the yellowed sheet that she had been covered with, not wanting it to be near her and curious about how many diseases it might carry. To describe the room as messy would be too polite. Shambolic hovel would be nearer the mark. She wondered how far gone she must have been to allow someone to bring her back to a dump like this. She looked down at herself and saw that she was at least still dressed. No sign of a roofie nightmare where someone had slipped something into a drink she may or may not have had. She realised she was getting off track again, and decided to focus on what she knew whilst she waited for the brain fog to clear and show her what she had done the previous night. She let her eyes take in the room the butterfly feeling in her stomach increasing in intensity the more she looked. Dirty floorboards spotted with old paint, the wood fibres rough and splintered, rusty nails holding them in place. The wallpaper sick and yellow, an ugly floral pattern which somehow looked loose on the wall, rippled with damp and mould. She saw a clear vision, a light in the fog of rotten skin sliding off a white bone skull and shuddered. The wallpaper was spotted with black mould which stretched up the walls like an alien landscape, thick and black in the spider web dusted corners. An old steel radiator sat under a window which was covered with a filthy makeshift curtain which looked like a sheet pinned up to keep out the light. A broken wardrobe sat in one corner, completely empty and missing its doors. There was a shade less light on the ceiling, the switch grubby and stained black, then the door. She looked at the bed, noting that it didn't look like one in which she had just gone through the throes of passion in. she was fully clothed, the other side of the grubby bed untouched and not slept in.

She started to wonder about the shitty condition of the room and wondered if the person who owned it had just moved in. Certainly, it looked that way and that they hadn't had time to renovate. She swung her legs off the side of the bed, grateful to find her shoes neatly placed next to it. Getting a splinter in her foot would be bad enough if the floor wasn't as filthy as it was. Something caught her eye as a spider, plump with long legs which shouldn't have been able to support its weight skittered across the edge of the room with what she perceived as urgency. It disappeared into the darkness under the wardrobe and once again she was alone. She slipped her feet into her shoes and stood, the bed creaking again in protest. The smell in the room was starting to bother her, the mildew stench burning her nostrils. She didn't know who she had come back with and the memories were slow to return. She did know, however that she wanted out and wanted out now.

She walked to the door, grimacing at the grimy handle. She twisted it, but the knob didn't move. She tried the opposite direction and tried to tell herself it was just jammed and that nobody would lock her in a place like this.

'Hello? Is anyone there?" she said, not quite shouting but still turning the handle in both directions as if the motion would free it. She was starting to panic, but wouldn't quite give herself over to it as she was sure it was just her paranoia and confusion at waking in such a strange environment with no recollection of how she had got there. She stopped twisting the door handle and listened, trying to focus past the pulsing headache and her anxious breathing.

Silence.

It felt to her as if there was nothing behind the door as if the rest of the world had ceased to exist apart from the room she was in. she walked to the window and pushed the makeshift curtain aside, squinting at the sunlight.

The window was barred and looked out onto a brick wall. She tried to pry it open, but the frames had been nailed shut and, like the rest of the room were covered in black mould, the glass hazy with condensation due to the poor ventilation. She returned to the door, panic fully setting in as she slammed her palms against the tired looking frame which was sturdier than it had first appeared.

'Can someone let me out of here? The door's stuck and I need to go home.'

Despite trying not to think about it, panic was definitely setting in. she had seen so many documentaries, so many films about people who were taken away and locked in rooms against their will although as was the case with society, things like that never happened to people like her. It was always someone else. The rational side of her mind said that it was just a coincidence and that the door was likely stuck and she would be laughing it away with her mystery one-night stand within minutes. Even so, until she was safe, she couldn't relax and so reverted to banging on the door and twisting the handle.

'Please, can anyone out there hear me?"

There was a sound, a distant thud of boots on steps coming towards her. She stood back, relieved and grateful to be getting out of the room and to freedom. The boots were louder now, echoing on bare wood as they came closer to the door.

'Sorry for the noise, it's just that the door seems to be stuck and I can't get out.' She called through to the other side as the owner of the boots stopped on the other side of the door. She heard a keychain rattle, the sound of key in a lock which at that moment she thought was the most glorious thing she had ever heard. However, the main door didn't open. Instead, a small hatch recessed into the bottom panel inched open. She stared at it as a plastic water bottle was rolled into the room, the door quickly closing again and being locked. She stared at the bottle, then at the door as the realisation hit her that she wasn't getting out of the room.

'Wait, didn't you hear me? Let me out? Whoever you are you can't just keep me here. Are you listening to me?" she started to bang on the door again, this time without fear of looking stupid. Her gut had tightened into a ball of fire as she screamed and slammed her fists on the door. Whoever was on the other side ignored her. She heard another rattle as the keychain was put away, then listened as the boots slowly made their way back down the steps, leaving her alone in her prison. When she had screamed herself hoarse and begrudgingly drunk from the offered bottle, she slid down into a sitting position, no longer caring about the cold clammy touch of mildew covered wallpaper on her skin or of the smell. All she wanted was to be home and away from whatever nightmare she had stumbled into. Across the room, the spider she had seen earlier reappeared from the darkness underneath the wardrobe and skittered to the other side of the room, keeping close to the dirt marbled skirting. She couldn't help but laugh. Both human and arachnid just as trapped and helpless as each other. With nothing else to do and her throat raw from exertion, she picked up the water bottle that had been put through the hatch and took a sip as she waited for her memories to return.

#3

NOW

The Club.

The man returned to where he had left Harley sitting at a corner booth. A quieter spot where they could talk without the need to shout. Smiling, he set the two drinks down on the table before he took his seat opposite from her. A vodka and orange for the lady and a whiskey for himself. What he didn't confess, though, was that her drink contained a double shot of spirits.

'You're still here!' he said as he made himself comfortable. 'I was worried you might have run off when my back was turned. Especially given the fact the queue was so slow over at the bar. Think they need to employ more staff given how...' He stopped himself. 'Sorry, I'm rambling. Ignore me.' He extended his hand. 'My name's Jacob,' he said.

Play nice.

'Harley.' She took his hand and they shook.

'Harley? Like the bike?' A sudden look of panic appeared on his face. 'Oh shit, that sounded so much better in my head. I didn't mean bike as in...

I meant… You know… Harley Davidson.' He tried to change the subject from his slip-up and asked, 'Your surname isn't Davidson, is it?'

'Yes.'

'Fuck off. Really?'

She laughed. 'No.' Her laugh was fake not that Jacob could tell. 'You didn't slip anything in this, did you?' she asked as she picked her drink up from the table with one hand. Her other hand, gripped the black plastic straw and moved it closer to her mouth. As she waited for an answer, she raised an eyebrow.

'Only ice-cubes and even then, it wasn't me. It was the bartender.'

Harley smiled at Jacob before sucking on the straw. Her eyes were fixed on his. His eyes were fixed on her mouth; her lips wrapped around the straw. She already knew the answer as to whether he had slyly dropped anything in her drink. She had watched him closely from where she was sitting at the booth. She set the drink back down on the table.

'So. How come you are here alone?'

'I was supposed to meet a friend here but they haven't shown up.'

'Some friend.'

'She was having family issues. I'm sure there is a good reason.' Harley changed the conversation from her to him. The less questions about her, the better. Especially given the fact she didn't have a complete back story - just snippets here and there. Enough, she hoped, to ensure she could get what she wanted. *Hoped?* She didn't understand why she was doubting herself. She had done this before - and not just once. She knew what she was doing. The men never really care that much about the women. They only ask enough questions to ensure they can progress things to the next stage with minimal fuss. They're all the same. Harley asked, 'So what about you? Where are your friends?'

'Well I thought we were coming out for a laugh and a few drinks but...' He laughed nervously as though he wasn't sure whether he should confess as to what had happened. He didn't want Harley thinking he was after the same as his friend. Although, the thought popped in his head, if it was offered... 'Okay let me just say that I'm talking to you because I liked the look of you and thought you looked lonely. Okay?' Harley frowned. Whatever this was, it was new. She sat back in her seat and waited for him to finish. He continued, 'The last I saw my friend, he was being led into the women's toilet by a little red-head.' Harley didn't look surprised. She hated the majority of men in places like this. 99.9% of them all seemed to have a one track mind when they came out on a Saturday night but that didn't make the women entirely innocent. Yes, some girls wanted to come out with their friends just to have a dance and let loose. De-stress from a hard working week. But there was no denying the fact that some girls were slags, plain and simple. Jacob reiterated, 'Like I said, that's not why I'm talking to you. I'm not expecting you to lead me through to the bathroom...'

'Glad to hear it!' Harley said. With the way Jacob had spoken Harley knew that, despite his protests, he would jump at the chance of being taken through to the bathroom for a quick fuck or suck. Most men would, even if they didn't openly fancy the woman offering. *Any hole's a goal.* 'Anyway,' Harley continued, 'I much prefer a bedroom. Less chance of being interrupted. Nothing worse than someone banging on the door just as you're about to climax.' Jacob spat a mouthful of whiskey back into his glass, surprised by her response. 'Oh come on,' Harley laughed, 'everyone likes to fuck, right?'

'Erm. Yes. I guess so.' Jacob mopped around his mouth with the back of his shirt sleeve. His face had reddened from the sudden change in Harley's character and the fact he'd made himself look stupid by spitting his drink out. 'Sorry. Just... Wasn't expecting you to say that.'

Harley smiled that fake smile again. 'Only human.' She hated talking like this. It wasn't her. She wasn't one of *those* girls flirting with the men down on the dance-floor or swallowing mouthfuls of cum in the dirty bathrooms. She was respectable. She had a good job, she earned a good wage, she came from a good family. This wasn't her. Usually. Tonight, it *had* to be her but it wasn't because she wanted it to be this way. It was for the greater good and - now - it was just a question of getting it over and done with. The sooner she started, the sooner it would be done and morning would be here with a new day and everything back to how it should be. Respectable. With a bubbling in the depths of her stomach, one she knew only too well, she swallowed back her pride and morals and asked, 'So really the question is - do we go back to your place?' It was a question Jacob had planned to ask. He smiled, happy that he had summoned the courage to talk to her in the first place. His friend was getting a quick suck and fuck in the shit-stained toilets and *he* was going to get a whole night of fun in the comfort of a bed. At least he could be getting that if it weren't for the fact...

'My place isn't free. What about yours?'

#4

BEFORE

The Room.

No help came.

She had no clue how long she had been in the room as there was no way for her to gauge the passing of time. She had waited for day turning into night to tell her, then realised that the window she had been given in the room wasn't as it seemed. It was all part of the room, the brick wall it looked out onto part of the setting. She could see the light bulbs set into the top of the wall above the outside of the window. As a tool to give the impression of light and space it served its purpose. It still didn't change the fact however that the room was windowless. She was also unsure now if she was upstairs or down. When she first heard Boots – the name she had given her mystery captor due to his heavy footfall- she had assumed he was coming upstairs to bring her food or water or to collect the bucket she was forced to use as a toilet. That was when she thought she had a window though and her frazzled brain had convinced her she was in an upper bedroom. Now she was more convinced she was downstairs. Somewhere underground where neither light nor her screams for help would penetrate.

Life had settled into a helpless routine. She existed in the room alone (apart from Steve – the name she had christened the spider who periodically appeared on his quest for flies and the cockroaches which were plentiful especially when her artificial daylight was extinguished, plunging the room into darkness. That was the worst part, listening to those night sounds in the pitch dark and wondering if the person holding her captive was coming to rape or kill her. None of that had, so far at least, happened. Her food and drink was pushed through the hatch in the door and collected again when she was finished. Always microwaveable ready meals or things that could be eaten cold. Never anything where she would need to use a knife or fork. Despite her sobs and pleading to be let free, she had never heard the person speak or heard them respond to her questions. She had now stopped trying to make contact and had instead kept herself busy as time crept by ever slower with trying to figure out a way to escape, a plan which she had quickly realised would require some kind of outside intervention. She had already disregarded the window as an option as even the glass wasn't as it seemed. It was a flexible kind of plastic which was impossible to break (she had tried). She had moved the furniture, turned the bed on its side, slid the wardrobe away from the wall and exposing a ghostly image of it on the wall penned in mould for her troubles and a few pellets on the floor which she suspected were mouse droppings (although mouse and access point had so far remained elusive). She had even gone around the room tapping the walls looking for weakness after remembering a film she had seen once where a guy had been wrongfully imprisoned and spent the next thirty years chipping away at his cell wall with a rock hammer as the concrete was weak.

She ignored the voice in her head that reminded her that she didn't have a rock hammer, nor did she want to spend the next thirty years digging her way into the unknown, and told it she would cross that bridge when she got to it. The argument quickly became invalid anyhow, as, despite the mould and the rot, the walls themselves were rock solid and showed no signs whatsoever of weakness. In the movies she liked to watch on a quiet Saturday night, the hero of the story in situations like this would devise their vengeance which we would have to duly wait until act three to witness. But they were gifted the props and loopholes that fiction demanded to make the reader pay their money to see the film, however in her situation there were no such needs, and so no plotting or scheming. No secretly making traps and weapons like John Rambo in First Blood as he waited to ambush Teasle and his men who you just knew were out of their depth against the retired Green Beret. All she had was time and the heady mixture of dread and anticipation about what would come next when her kidnapper (she had come to terms with calling him or her that) chose to present themselves. With the passage of time, she began to wonder if there was a master plan for her. If there was any next phase of the story since she had been taken.

The person who had taken her could be another Joseph Fritzel although he was more hands on and impregnated his own daughters and made them give birth to his children. Her current situation was entirely different in that she didn't feel in any immediate danger apart from those terrifying hours when the lights went out and she could hear the sounds in the night of the cockroaches moving around or what she presumed to be her so far elusive mice guests scratching in the walls. It was during those times in the absolute pitch dark that she felt most exposed. Sleep was spotty at best, and she had taken to getting the bulk of her rest during the day, napping lightly whilst still keeping her awareness of the surroundings should anyone come into the room. The periods of darkness were tense never ending passages of fear where every sense was attuned to her surroundings. And yet, still nobody came. She lay now on the bed, pillow folded under her, arms behind her head (funny how a person can get used to their environment so quickly) and was trying to piece together how she had come to be held prisoner. The soup in her brain on that first day hadn't lifted in a sense that she still had no recollection of events leading up to her waking in the room she had been in ever since.

The last clear memory she had was of a taxi and her getting in it. There was no memory of a destination or why she was even in there in the first place, she did know it was the memory from just before she had woken up in the room though as she was wearing the same clothes. She sighed and tried to force her memory to pull the sequence of events out, but there was nothing there. The feeling was akin to having a name on the tip of the tongue and being unable to recall it. All she could remember was the taxi. Like the outside of the room, she was in, everything else before and after didn't seem to exist. She sighed and closed her eyes, hoping to try and get some sleep before the lights went out.

#5

NOW

The Taxi.

Harley slid over to the far side of the back taxi-seat before Jacob climbed in next to her, pulling the door closed when he could.

'Where to, buddy?'

Jacob looked at Harley who smiled seductively at him. She licked her lips as she twirled a lock of her long brown hair around her index finger. Jacob smiled, still amazed that he was going home with this beautiful woman. Well, not home. His home *wasn't* free, just as he had told her back in the club. Sadly, neither was her place and so... 'Nearest vacant hotel would be good,' he said.

'There's a Premier Inn about ten minutes away. Not sure if they have vacancy but can check there if you want? It's more or less on the way to other hotels anyway. Unless, of course, you had something a little more *exclusive* in mind?'

'Premier Inn sounds good to me, so long as it has a bed.'

'I hear that, buddy. Hell of a long day. Still got three hours left yet before I call it a night.' Jacob looked at Harley and rolled his eyes. The last thing he wanted right now was a chatty cab driver when he had a hot girl to be talking to. Harley just laughed. A genuine laugh this time. She didn't care if she had ten minutes of not having to talk to Jacob. In an ideal world, she would have longer still. A gripe in her stomach reminded her that this wasn't an ideal world. A second gripe followed quickly and the smile faded from her face as she wished the cab driver would put his foot down. 'Saturdays are always busy. Not so bad earlier in the evening but by the early hours you tend to get the weirdos and drunks, you know?'

'Can't say that I do.'

'Doing this job, you see some things!'

'Look, I'm sorry and I don't mean to be rude but I kind of want to talk to my lady-friend. That okay?'

The taxi driver shot him a look via the rear-view mirror. *Fuck you.* 'Sure, buddy, whatever floats your boat.' The driver turned his attention back to the road, ignoring his fare. Jacob turned to Harley holding in his laughter. He hadn't meant to offend the driver but - at the same time - he didn't actually give a shit. Chances of seeing this driver again were remote. He still hoped he had a chance to see Harley again. Anyway, it wasn't a long journey, he was sure the driver would be okay to not talk for a while. He could always give the next fare his life story...

'I take it the Premier Inn is okay with you?' Jacob asked Harley having realised he hadn't even checked with her. She might have been expecting something posher, something more exclusive - such as *The Shangri-La* at *The Shard,* a truly amazing hotel which Jacob had had the pleasure of staying in once before. As much as he would love to stay there again this evening, there was no way he could afford it this close to the end of the month (and before pay day) and whilst the room payment hadn't been discussed, he was pretty sure he would be picking up both the tab for that and the ride there. Looking at how beautiful Harley was, though, it was the least he could do. Harley answered him with a simple nod of her head. Jacob laughed, 'Can't believe we're doing this. I know you probably won't believe me but, yeah, this isn't something I tend to make a habit of.' Harley looked at him as though she didn't believe him; raised eyebrows. In fairness to Jacob, what he said was true though, he didn't make a habit of going home with women he had only just met. It wasn't because he didn't want to. It was more to do with the fact he wasn't very good at talking to women, not without a first introduction anyway and - in places like the club - his friends were more interested in setting themselves up, not with helping him out.

Jacob noticed the taxi driver was giving him a funny look in the rear-view mirror for a second time. He tried to ignore him and focused on Harley instead. She was still looking at him with an expression of disbelief on her face. He laughed. 'I knew you wouldn't believe me...' Uncomfortable with Harley's silence, and the fact the driver kept looking at him - was he laughing at him? - he fell quiet and let the drone of the engine fill the awkward silence. In the back of his mind, he wondered whether this was the worst taxi-ride in the history of dire rides. Harley, on the other hand, knew that it wasn't. There had been worse rides. Far worse.

#6

BEFORE

Locked Doors.

When memory returned it was a sudden thing. There was no forewarning, no gradual lifting of the veil. She had been on her bunk listening to the roaches scurry around, a sound that had gone from one that repulsed her to one that comforted her and let her know she wasn't alone. She remembered the taxi ride in detail now, everything from the red glow of the door lock light to the strange feeling she had got from the driver. It had all seemed fine at the time and certainly had given her no cause for concern. She had got in and given the directions of where she wanted to go. She remembered catching him watching her through the rearview mirror and subconsciously pulling her clothes closer to cover her body, but even then sensed no danger. Not really. She just assumed he was enjoying the view, one perk of what she assumed to be a dull and monotonous job. She had looked out of the window, trying to ignore the rearward glare and stared at row after row of darkened houses as those beyond slept. She was looking forward to getting home and taking her shoes off. They were new and had been pinching her toes all night. Her turn off was coming up, and she was planning what to make for a snack when the taxi drove straight past her street.

'You missed the turning. That was my street.' She waited for the reply or apology, but those eyes flicked to her then back to the road, ignoring her.

'Hey, did you hear me?' She knew he had, or course. Even through the Perspex divider designed to protect the driver from rowdy passengers. Yet still he didn't speak. 'Alright, it doesn't matter. Just stop here and I'll walk the rest of the way.' Still no response. The driver turned left, then took a right, moving further away from her house and banishing any notion that it may be an error or oversight. 'Stop the car. Let me out right now.' She planned to say it without panic, but her voice still came out strained and high pitched. The rearview mirror eyes flicked to her again and creased at the edges. She couldn't see the drivers face but she knew he was smiling. She tried the door handle, pulling at it and banging on the window. But the little red light indicator that said the doors were locked stopped her escape, and there was little to no traffic to catch the attention of. She stood in the back of the taxi, hunched over and half stepped towards the Perspex divider between front and back of the cab. 'Let me go, just stop here and let me out. If you're trying to scare me it worked. Please just-B...' The last words didn't come out. Even though the road was clear the driver slammed on the brakes, launching her forward and smashing her face against the Perspex. She fell to the floor in the back of the taxi, nose stinging and eyes watering.

They were already on their way again.

Phone.

Phone for help.

She clambered back onto the seat watching as the city fell away and they moved into a quieter area where moonlit fields and trees became the dominant features of the landscape. Her hands were shaking and tears blurred her vision as she took her phone out of her bag and unlocked it. She hesitated, unsure who to call. The police would be the obvious choice, but she had no idea how to describe where she was. The taxi had no numbers, no identifying marks to help her tell someone. And besides, she knew the driver would do something if he saw her making a call. Instead, she went to the text message section, picking out her mother's number. *Help me. In taxi and driver won't let me out. Not sure where I am. Call police.* She stopped typing. The driver had stopped the car, pulling over in a leafy lay-by shrouded by trees and overlooking cornfields which danced and swam as if alive under the moonlight. She was too afraid to move. She could only sit there and watch as he got out of the car and walked to the rear door and opened it.

'Please, I don't want any trouble,' she said as he leaned in. 'just let me go and-' he punched her hard, catching her flush on the jaw and snapping her head back, in doing so banishing the world and her problems and replacing it with a silent landscape of absolute black.

#7

NOW

The Two of Them.

Jacob checked them into the room as Harley hung back, waiting by a coffee machine in the lobby. Jacob presumed she was just embarrassed, perhaps worried the receptionist might ask questions that she wouldn't know the answer to. Maybe a question which would highlight the fact they weren't a real couple and were there for nothing more than a cheap night of drunken sex. Not that Jacob nor Harley were particularly drunk.

'Thank you,' said Jacob as he took the room keys; small plastic credit cards in a cardboard sleeve - one for him and one for her. The woman smiled and continued the admin work Jacob had interrupted her from when he had first approached. 'Ready?' he asked Harley as he headed towards the lift. She smiled (fake) and nodded as she joined him. He leaned towards the call button for the elevator and pressed it once, illuminating the light. 'You're my wife tonight,' Jacob mused. Harley looked at him, confused. 'I didn't know what else to say when I was checking us in. It was the first thing that popped in my head.' He looked at her. 'Is that weird?' He didn't wait for Harley to answer him. 'It is a bit. This is why I've been single for so long.' Much to his relief, the elevator doors opened allowing him the chance to escape his own awkward conversation. The pair of them stepped in and the doors closed. Jacob pressed the number "3" on the control panel and leant back with his back pressed against the wall. He was excited, that went without saying, but the closer he got - the more nervous he felt. He blamed Harley's sudden change in personality on this. One minute she was quiet, the next she was teasing him and - now - she was quiet again. Quite simply, he didn't know where he stood. Did she want to be there or not? From the corner of his eye, he noticed Harley rub her stomach as though in discomfort. 'You okay?' he asked.

She lied, 'Just nervous.'

'Really?'

'Well - like you said - I don't make a habit of this,' she said. Another lie. Her words surprised him. She was the one who had been so forward with him in the club. And this - checking in at the hotel - had been her idea too. He just hadn't argued. 'I thought I was the nervous one.' The lift doors opened at the requested floor. Jacob motioned for Harley to lead the way. *Ever the gentleman.* He realised she didn't know the room number and - therefore - didn't know the direction to turn. 'To the left,' he said. He stepped out of the elevator and turned left, stepping in front of Harley in order to lead her to the room. 'This way.'

#8

BEFORE

The Wash-Room.

He opened the door.

She hadn't expected it, and despite in the waking terrors she experienced he always came at night when it was at its most dark, it was when the lights were on, that the door lock opened. He stood there at the threshold, staring at her the eyes familiar from the taxi. In her mind, she had built him up as a monster, a twisted, horrifically scarred beast. In reality, he was just a man. A big man, granted, his grubby mustard polo shirt stretched over his immense gut, oversized baggy jeans hanging from him badly and making him look mismatched. His head was bald, his face pitted and lined like old leather. She pushed herself back against the bedstead, terrified of what was to come. He tossed something into the room, two objects which landed on the bottom of the bed.

'Wash.' He said his voice like gravel.

She looked at the cloth and towel on the bed then at the man.

'Why have you taken me? Who are you keeping me here? I just want to go home.'

'Wash'. He said again and pointed to the open door. His eyes were like those of a doll or a shark. She saw no compassion, no humanity within them. Although she was afraid, it seemed this was a chance to get out of the room and at least look at the rest of the building. Perhaps that would give her the opportunity to get away and find her way to freedom. She got off the bed, fighting her every instinct which told her to stay away from the man. She remembered reading somewhere that it made it difficult for a captor to hurt a victim if they were humanised and thought it was worth a shot.

'Do you have a name? my name is Cherrelle?' she forced herself to try and meet his gaze, but the man seemed to look through her as if she were another dilapidated piece of furniture in the room.

'Yeah, I have a name. Now wash.'

'Please, why are you doing this to me? Why can't you just let me go?' He gave her a look, one which told her it was time to be quiet. She grabbed the washcloth and towel from the foot of the bed and walked towards him. Up close she could see how big he was. His skin was peppered with old acne scars and as she drew close she could smell the stale odour of old sweat. She approached the door, suddenly frightened about leaving the confines of the room that she had grown to consider safe. In a way, she thought it would have been easier if he had been a monster. At least then she would have the ability to feel hate. As it was, looking at a regular man, she was more curious than outright scared. 'Which way do I go?' she said at the door. She could see a slab of yellowed wallpaper and bare floor in the space outside the room. The man pointed down the hall.

'End door. Don't try anything stupid like running or you'll be sorry.' There it was. The threat and confirmation that the situation was much worse than she had anticipated. She inched out of the room, hating standing so close to him. He took her by the arm, his fingers digging into her flesh as he led her to the bathroom. One thing at least was answered. It was clear by the concrete walls and mould covered storage boxes that her room was in the cellar. She could see a wooden staircase winding out of sight to the upper floors of the house and whatever they might hold. Heeding the man's words and too afraid to disobey them she walked past the staircase and the freedom beyond to the only other door. She pushed it open and stopped on the threshold. The room was no larger than a closet and had been converted into a makeshift bathroom, she guessed for this exact purpose. She wondered, in the back of her mind, how many others before her had gone through this routine. The room contained a filthy toilet without a seat, the porcelain covered in limescale and stains where it had never been cleaned. The rim was lined with dirt and hairs and the rear pipes at floor level were shrouded in cobwebs. The stench hit her, a foul ammonia smell that burned her nose. Other than the toilet, there was a shower head which had been badly erected on the wall. It was covered in rust and its face was coated in rust. A mildew coated curtain was pulled back and a single small drain hole set in the floor. 'Go on. Wash.' The man said again.

She knew what would come next. He would wait until she got undressed then rape her. Maybe even kill her. She tensed, waiting for him to lunge. Instead of attacking, the man stepped back.

'Don't do anything stupid. I'll wait outside.' He said, then closed the door, leaving her alone in the stinking cubicle room. She stood there, heart thundering and wondering just how she was going to get out of this situation. Even so, she needed to wash. She had been in the same clothes since she had arrived and could smell the filth on herself. She switched on the tower, the unseen pipes groaning as they spat out tepid water which was little more than a trickle. She looked at the door, straddling the line between compliance and fight, then chose the former. She needed to clean herself up and she reasoned that if he was feeding her and giving her these most basic of human rights that he may not hurt her yet. Although it went against her every instinct, she undressed and pulled the curtain closed. She washed, moving quickly, senses attuned for the sound of the door opening and the man coming in when she was at her most vulnerable, but neither thing happened. She dried off and dressed then exited the room. The man was sitting on the steps, watching her. 'Back in the room.' he said. She hesitated, not wanting to be locked back in that place. She was desperate to get home. By now people would be worried and looking for her, especially after the text she had sent.

'Please, just let me go. I won't tell anyone about this place I promise.'

'Don't make me ask you again. Back in the room.'

She looked beyond the man on the steps and her mind swam with the possibilities of what might await her if she could only get past him. As if reading her thoughts, the man half-smiled.

'If you're thinking of doing something stupid right now, you might want to reconsider.'

'I... I wasn't.' she said, hating that dead look in his eye.

'Good. Then back in the room.'

She started to walk, conscious of him following her. 'I don't understand this. I don't know you. What did I do to deserve this? I have a family. They'll be looking for me.'

'They won't find you.'

The cold indifference in which he said the words hit her hard. Her stomach tightened and she was sure she was going to throw up. They had reached the threshold of her room. A little while ago she was reluctant to leave it, but seeing it now, so cold and uninviting, she didn't want to go back in. she turned to face the man, knowing it was stupid and could cost her. 'Look, let's just talk. Maybe I can help you maybe I can...' he shoved her. Not hard, but with intent. She staggered back and was once again in her cell. He looked her up and down, eyes still devoid of anything resembling humanity.

'I'll bring food soon.' He said, then closed the door. She listened to the sound of the lock turning then his footsteps as he walked away. With nothing else to do she threw herself on the bed and cried.

#9

NOW

Stalling.

Harley had excused herself the moment they got to the hotel room. She headed through to the bathroom as Jacob started to look around the room to see what was what. There was a double bed, comfortable enough. There was a writing desk and, piled up on it, booklets detailing what the hotel offered. A medium-sized television, flatscreen, hung from the wall. There was a wardrobe. Inside the wardrobe were coat hangers that were actually attached to the clothes rail in there so people couldn't steal them. Jacob laughed to himself, *did people really steal coat hangers*? He continued looking around the rather small room. Two bedside cabinets, either side of the bed, one of which being empty and the other home to a hardback edition of *The Bible*. Back across the other side of the room and - ah ha - tea and coffee making equipment tucked away on a shelf within the wardrobe. He knew it would be there somewhere. He didn't make a habit of staying in hotel rooms but, even so, he knew they usually had a small kettle somewhere around. A small kettle and a selection of different styles of tea.

Even better, two packets of biscuits. Cookies, to be precise. He took the tray, including the kettle and various bits and pieces, from the shelf and put it on the table next to where the television hung. No doubt one of them would want a hot drink at some point and he had nothing else to do. *What was she doing in there?*

'You okay in there?' he called through to the bathroom without moving from where he was standing by the table. He could hear her in there, shuffling around, but had no idea what she was doing although his first thought was *stomach issues* given the way she had been rubbing her stomach in the elevator. If that were the case, though, she wouldn't be moving around so much in there.

'I'll be right out,' she called back. The tone in her voice, she sounded as though she were okay. Certainly didn't sound as though she were in pain, or straining to get her body out of a narrow window - a great escape being his second thought.

'Did you want a hot drink? There's a kettle in here.' He called through not realising that, if she were to say 'yes', he had no way of filling the kettle until she reappeared anyway. There was no answer. The bathroom door's lock clicked back and the door opened as Jacob struggled with opening one of the tea packets (English Breakfast). Even if she didn't want one, he was a little parched and he didn't fancy paying over the odds to get room service to bring him the beer he actually craved.

'What do you think?' Harley stepped out of the bathroom. Jacob turned to her and his mouth fell agape. His eyes fixed to her naked body. She had a perfect hourglass figure that most girls would be envious of. Large breasts with nipples erect, already standing to attention. Her pubic hair had been completely shaven away. A look in her pretty, brown eyes suggested pure lust. Once again the shy girl was gone and the confident man-eater was back, taking Jacob by surprise for the second time. 'Well?' Leaning against the wall with one arm outstretched, a slight arch in her back, her fingernails drummed impatiently against the wooden frame of the door.

Jacob stuttered, 'W-Wow.' He cleared his throat. 'You look amazing.'

Harley smiled at his reaction. The night was getting close to the part she liked. Lull them into a false sense of security. Make them believe they're going to get something that isn't actually going to happen. Let them get their hopes up and then piss all over them. First though, she had to let them close. This was the part of the night she wasn't so keen on. The only benefit being in that it was over quickly. Usually. Ignoring the slow building pain in her stomach she stepped away from the doorway and approached Jacob.

Without realising what he was doing, he responded by taking a step backwards, bumping into the table. He had nowhere else to go as Harley reached him and put her arms around his shoulders. She pulled him close and kissed him passionately on the mouth. Her tongue explored his mouth, stroking his own tongue, and - as she pressed her body against his - she could feel the bulge in his trousers grow. She pulled away and smiled in the knowledge that he was hers now. He was grinning like an idiot. *The cat had got the cream.*

'I'm sorry,' he said, 'I still can't believe this is happening. When I approached you I never thought... I mean I wanted... I just thought there was no way. You're so pretty. Completely out of my league...' Had this been a normal pick-up with no ulterior motives, this would be where Jacob started to talk his way out of a hook-up because of his lack of confidence. He laughed. 'If only my friend could see...' Harley silenced him with another deep kiss. He put his hands around her waist before moving them to her pert buttocks. Inside, she was dying. She wanted to stop what she was doing and scream at him to get off. She didn't though. She continued playing the part he sought. He pulled away. 'You're fucking amazing.'

Harley pulled away from him, taking a step back. Her eyes were fixed on his but his were all over her body, exploring every inch of skin on show -

a smile still on his face. 'Take your clothes off.' It wasn't a request. It was an order from a woman taking control and seizing what she wanted.

'Maybe we could slow things down a little?' Jacob asked. His words caught Harley by surprise. Of all the men she'd done this with, so many filthy hands upon her body, she had never had one ask to slow things down. If anything, they were undressing *her* before she had a chance to strip off in the bathroom. A bubbling in her gut reminded her that she didn't have time to take things slower. This needed to happen if she were to feel any sort of relief. And justice. 'I mean, I don't really know you but - from what I do know - I like you. Might be nice to get to know each other a little first and then... I don't know... Just thought it might make it more... Nice. You know... When we...' Harley frowned.

'You don't want to fuck me?'

'No. Yes. No. I mean I want to get to know you and... I want to be with you, if you know what I mean.' He felt his face redden. 'I'm sorry, I'm making this awkward, aren't I?'

'I thought you wanted a fuck. The way you approached me...'

'I do. I mean. I want *more* than a...' He tried to explain himself better, 'I'm not used to one night stands. This is all new to me. I just thought we could get to know each other a little. I mean, if there was an option for it to turn into something more than a one night stand, I wouldn't mind seeing what happened...' Harley shook her head. 'No? No what? No it can't be more than a one night stand?'

'This is it.'

'I just think if you got to know me. You might feel a little differently.'

Harley sat on the edge of the bed. The stirring in her stomach was almost crippling and she was struggling to hide it from him. She didn't want anything more from him and she had realised she had brought the wrong man back with her. But she had started now. She had started and she needed to see it through. She didn't have a choice. She told herself that it would be okay once he started anyway. Once she got him to *that* point she wouldn't care and he would be the same as the other men before him. She just needed to get him to that point. Get any introductions he wanted to make out of his head. But then - maybe if she allowed him a quick introduction she might be able to get things back on track? *A compromise.* 'You want to tell me about yourself?' she asked him.

'And I want you to tell me about yourself.'

'I'm feeling a little underdressed. How about you take some of those clothes off and we lie on the bed. Then, we can cuddle up while we talk?'

She smiled (fake) sweetly at him. Her gut spasmed internally. 'A compromise.'

He smiled. After a slight pause he nodded. 'Seems fair.' Harley laid back on the bed with her legs slightly parted, giving him the enticing view of her wet (lube) cunt, as she watched him slowly peel his clothes from his body.

'Tell me about yourself.' She purred (acting) as her left hand moved between her legs and two fingers danced over her clitoris.

#10

BEFORE

Introductions.

The next time the man opened the door he brought a chair. He entered the room, set the grubby dining chair next to the bed and sat. For a while, neither of them spoke. They simply looked at each other. She was afraid, but so used to the feeling she presented it as indifference as she stared at the man who had ripped her from the life she had known and brought her to this place. The man looked awkward and desperately uncomfortable. She imagined he was lonely and had gone to extreme lengths to make sure he had a companion.

'I'm not a monster.'

She was surprised at this. He had never tried to open dialogue with her before, and she felt that all too familiar feeling of ice forming in the pit of her stomach. She looked at him without reply, getting a little pleasure from just how uncomfortable her silence was making him. He went on, stumbling over his words. 'I mean, I understand how this might look, but it's.... it's not what you think. My name is Edward.'

She glared at him, anger welling up and mixing with the fear in an explosive and intoxicating combination. 'You choose to introduce yourself now after, what five days? Six of me being here?"

'Twelve. Twelve days.' He said.

Twelve days. She hadn't realized that it had been so long. With no ability to keep track of time she knew she had been just guessing the days, but to find out twelve had passed was a shock.

'You're not saying much.' He said, those dead eyes crawling all over her.

'What do you want me to do? Thank you for kidnapping me and keeping me in this shit-hole?'

'It wasn't meant to be like this. I want us to be friends.'

'Fuck you.'

A shadow of something passed over his face. Fear, rage shock. He shifted position on his seat. 'You can't talk to me like that. Not in my house.'

'And you can't hold me here against my will.' She snapped, ignoring the possible consequences.

'You are supposed to be nice to me. I'm a man. Man dominates woman. That's how nature intended it.'

‘Oh, so you’re one of those chauvinist types. Well listen, you have no right to hold me here and no power over me. If you’re going to kill me, then kill me. If you’re not then let me go, just decide one way or the other because I’m sick of this.’ She was surprised by her own outburst. Under normal circumstances, she would never have said such things, but the conditions of her incarceration had made her stronger somehow, more determined to see the sun again and get out of the situation. Her instinct told her that this man was weak and although no doubt physically strong, he was mentally fragile. She had already committed to the idea that breaking him mentally was her best chance. She looked at him, staring at her, his mouth partially open in shock. ‘What? You didn’t expect me to fight? Did you think I’d just play the victim and let you do what you wanted with me? Fuck that. No man controls me. Either let me go or do what you are going to do.’

He stood, the chair tipping back and hitting the floor. He stared at her and for a horrible sick second she was sure she had made a terrible mistake. His mouth moved but no words came. She watched as he balled his fists at his sides. She knew now was the time to push if she intended to break him.

‘What’s wrong? Not used to being talked to like that, are you? What’s wrong? Did mummy neglect you? Did daddy touch you in your private places and ask you not to tell anyone? Is that how you grew up to be a fuck-up who kidnaps women and holds them hostage?'

'Stop it. Don't say that.'

'That's it isn't it. You know, at first, I thought you were going to rape me and wondered why you hadn't.I get it now though. You can't, can you? You probably can't get it up without thinking about daddy putting his mouth on it and warning you not to cum until he was ready or he'd beat the shit out of you. Am I right?'

He took a step back, almost tripping over the fallen chair. Anger throbbed in her like a rotten tooth. She climbed off the bed, getting in his face. 'I get it now. You're a pathetic little man with a pathetic little broken dick who gets his kicks doing this.'

'You'll regret saying that. You'll regret it.' he repeated it over and over under his breath but kept backing away from her.

She would have continued on, but he was already out of the room and was closing the door. She stayed where she was listening as he fumbled the keys, dropped them then scooped them up again and locked the door. She picked up the chair he had knocked over and sat down, confident that she had broken him and that it was only a matter of time before he either let her go or she just walked out without him stopping her. For the first time since she had been taken, she had hope.

#11

NOW

Fly to a Web.

Harley was listening to Jacob tell her his life story. She was on the bed, lying on her side still naked. He was on his back wearing only his socks and boxer shorts, too embarrassed or shy to get naked completely. He had just come out of a long-term relationship with a woman who had cheated on him. Harley could tell by the expression on his face that he regretted bringing up his past girlfriend the moment her name, Lucy, escaped his lips and yet he didn't stop or change the subject. He carried on explaining what had happened and the aftermath. The aftermath being that he struggled to trust women, too afraid to even talk to them for fear of getting hurt again. Harley was the first girl he had spoken to - the first stranger anyway - with the intention of trying to chat them up. He had explained he felt the whole approach awkward and was surprised she had even agreed to a drink with him. Surprised and thankful. He was a sweet guy, Harley could tell that, but that didn't mean he was a *good* guy. He deserved what was coming. The way she saw it, if he was a good guy, he would have asked for her phone number and asked her out on a real date later instead of agreeing to go back with her. Not that she could have dated him. She knew she couldn't date anyone ever again. That lifestyle was dead. As for Jacob, though, he wasn't as bad as some of the men she had met but his intentions were still questionable, despite what he was saying. Jacob suddenly laughed, snatching Harley away from her thoughts.

'I'm sorry. I'm not very good at this.' It was a fair statement. Accurate. Had this been a real coming together of two sexually frustrated people, he would be doing a great job of killing any chance for a pleasurable encounter. He might have been coming across as a friendly, sweet guy but that was it. He certainly wasn't making himself look sexually attractive to Harley with his tales of romance woe. She didn't mind though. None of the men were sexually attractive to her. That was why she had the small sachet of lubricant in her purse; to help take the sting away when... 'Ignore me,' he continued. Desperate to get things moving, she leaned over him and kissed him passionately again. He responded, as did his cock which started to harden once again, the more her tongue explored his mouth. She placed her hand over his genitals and gently rubbed, encouraging him to become fully erect. 'That feels nice,' he said when Harley pulled away from the shared kiss.

'Yeah?'

'Yes.'

'What about if I do this?' She reached into his shorts and gripped his cock before pulling it free from the cotton. Her other hand moved the shorts down to just below his testicles as she slowly stroked him up and down, up and down. Her thumb teased the eye of his dick which was already wet from pre-cum. *He isn't a good guy.* 'Do you want me to suck it?' she asked. She knew that if he went along with it, she would have him exactly where she wanted and there would be fuck all he could do.

'Yes.'

'How badly?'

'Badly. I want you so fucking badly. I want to be inside you.' There was a strong tone of desperation in Jacob's voice. Harley knew that, if they fucked as he wanted, then he would most likely be taking charge of the situation. Perhaps starting off in missionary with her pinned beneath. That's how most of them liked to start, back when she first started doing *this*. They would start with missionary and then get bored before flipping her onto all fours or slamming her against a wall and fucking her up against it hard. The problem with all of those positions was that, she wasn't in a position to stop them from running when her true intentions were revealed.

They could just pull out and make a dash for the door. Not that they ever made it through it. Even so, it was easier if she could retain the control and trap them so they weren't able to move much at all. The way Jacob sighed when he spoke, she knew she had to take charge of the situation before he did. 'You can't just rush into that, baby. You need a little foreplay.' She reiterated, 'You can't rush it. It's better to build it up slow.'

#12

BEFORE

Fucked.

She was wrong.

More wrong than she had ever been in her life. She had been dozing as she did during the day, straddling the line between sleep and consciousness, in limbo and imagining her friends and family and all the things she was going to do when she was free. This was a second chance, an opportunity to right the wrongs after surviving such an ordeal which she had been convinced would happen since her encounter with the man a few hours earlier. Part of her had felt guilty at how merciless she had been, then she remembered that he was the one who had kidnapped her and was holding her against her will. She never imagined what would happen next.

Footsteps on floorboards, a familiar sound when he brought her food or changed her bucket (neither of which he had done for two days since their standoff. She presumed as a form of punishment.) but arriving with more urgency than usual. She was still in that half sleep state, though, and so failed to register the danger even when the door was thrown open. It wasn't until she felt him grab her by the hair and yank her onto the floor did she realise how very, very wrong she had been. He threw her into the corner and she screamed. He still held a handful of her hair in his fist as she lay against the wall confused and struggling to catch her breath. The meek, broken man from a few days ago was gone and had been replaced by a naked monster whose arousal was obvious to see. He kicked her hard in the stomach, banishing both breath and any idea of putting up a fight.

'You cunt bitch. Ridicule me in my own house?' he grunted as he grabbed her by the hair again and pulled her to her feet. She clawed and scratched at his eyes, but her fighting seemed to excite him. He punched her in the face, her nose exploding, her teeth cracking. She screamed, spitting blood and a broken tooth onto the filthy floor. He threw her onto the bed and clambered on top of her, wrapping one massive hand around her throat.

'That's the trouble with you fucking feminists. You never know when to shut your hole. Well, I'll give you something for those holes, both of them'.

He was panting and sweating, but his eyes were just as black and lifeless as before. She knew what was about to happen to her and was completely powerless to stop it. She was sure her nose was broken and she could only breathe in ragged gasps through her broken mouth. With his free hand, he reached down and ripped off her shirt, exposing her bra.

'Look at those tits. I could suck on em' for a week.' He grunted as he pawed at them over her bra, sweat dripping off the end of his nose and onto her face. She was sobbing, everything that was happening both horrifically real and somehow alien to her. She tried to squirm away from him but he tightened his grip on her throat.

'Don't do that. You get what's coming to you and you enjoy it.'

She screamed again and he grinned. 'Scream all you like, cunt. Nobody will hear you down here.' He slipped his free hand down past the front of her jeans. She squirmed again and he tightened his grip on her neck. 'I'm doing this no matter if you are conscious or not. It makes no difference to me.'

She stopped struggling, wincing as he probed inside her. 'See? You act like you don't like it but you're wet in there.' he grunted, foul breath on her face as he pushed first three then all four fingers in. 'let's warm you up, just so you're ready for me.'

He had big hands and his actions hurt. Whenever she tried to squeeze her legs closed to stop him he squeezed her neck harder. When he had done, he pulled his hand out and flipped her over so she was face down on the bed. She cried, burying her face in the filthy pillow as he pulled her jeans down. 'Look at that lovely arse of yours. I'm going to fuck that so hard. So so hard,' he grunted in her ear as he lay on top of her and pushed himself inside her. She screamed, the pain intense and unlike anything she had ever felt before. He didn't seem to mind and wedged himself deeper into her anus. 'That's it. You love it don't you, cunt'. He pulled her hair back as he thrust. And forced his still wet fingers into her mouth. 'Go on, taste your own pussy. You cunts love it I bet,' he said as he put all his weight on her. She lay there, humbled and humiliated and hoped it would be over quickly, but he was machine like and showed no sign of stopping. He withdrew from her then flipped her over again onto her front. He slapped her hard, then pawed at her breasts pulling her nipples until she screamed in pain and leaving them purple and bruised.

'Now you're going to suck this shit off my cock,' he said, pulling her into a sitting position and standing by the bed. 'If you bite it or try to hurt me, I'll kill you.'

She wanted to beg and plead for him not to, but he had already pulled her head forward and shoved it into her mouth, forcing himself as far back into her throat as he could go. He grabbed her by the back of the head and pulled her head towards him as he pushed. She gagged, bloody drool dripping onto the mattress. She couldn't breathe, her mangled nostrils closed and not working, her airway blocked. She started to claw at him, desperate for breath.

'You love this, don't you, cunt,' he said as he pulled her hair harder as he pushed himself further in. she wanted to gag but was unable to get the leverage to breathe. When it felt certain she was going to die he pulled her back, allowing her to take a bloody gasp as great saliva strands dangled from her chin and onto her chest. He hit her again, light exploding as his fist connected with her cheek and sending her crashing back down onto the bed.

'I'm ready to come now, bitch. You're going to take all of it.' He tore off her jeans, pulling them aside and pushing her legs open. 'Look at that gash, just gaping there all for me.' He pushed his fingers in again this time almost forcing a knuckle in there to a chorus of screams. 'Can't fit it in. too tight.' He clambered on top of her, massive body pinning her down. She barely felt him enter her. By then she had switched off and blacked out what was happening, her body alive with pain and fear. She hated herself for not fighting, for allowing him to do it, but even so he hit her. She felt him bite her nipples as he thrust piston-like into her as if he would never stop.

'Not long now,' he grunted, his flabby body covered with sweat as he increased the velocity of his motion. He wrapped both hands around her throat, squeezing as he moved faster. She coughed and gagged, spitting blood and drool out onto her cheeks.

‘That’s it. Almost...almost...’

She felt consciousness fading, dimly aware of the hot sticky rush as he climaxed inside her. By then it was a distant thing as the light faded from her world and the terrors that were in it became a distant memory.

#13

NOW

Teasing.

Still lying next to Jacob, Harley smiled. It wasn't a fake smile. This one was genuine. *He isn't a good guy. He's just like the rest of them.* Desperate to fuck her. He was going to get what he deserved. She looked down to the erection still in her hand, not because she wanted to get a better look at it - she just didn't want him seeing the grimace on her face as another cramping rattled her insides. *It will stop soon. It will all be over.* Until the next time, that is, and they seem to be getting closer and closer together. Harley jolted as her pussy suddenly pulsed. It was time. She was ready. She just needed to get in position. Sitting up, she looked back at Jacob and winked at him with a cheeky (fake) smile. He smiled back as she shifted position so that her head was next to his hard-on and her arse was pointed towards the head of the bed. 'Did you want me to suck it?' she asked. She was referring to Jacob's cock. When she spoke, he could feel her warm breath against it.

'Yes,' he sighed in anticipation. His member twitched, also in anticipation.

'Beg.'

'Please.'

'That's not begging. Beg for it.'

'Please. Please suck my cock. I'll do anything.'

'Anything?'

'Yes.' His erection twitched again. 'Anything. Just please put it in your mouth.' He couldn't recall the last time he had a woman being this forward with him, completely unaware that she had no intention of putting her mouth anywhere near his shaft. It was just a way of getting him where she needed him. A way of stopping him from pushing her away and running. 'Please suck it.'

'Only if you lick me.'

'Okay.'

'I want to feel your tongue deep inside me.'

'Sit on my face!' He was breathing heavily. The thought of her sucking him off was driving him wild, so wild in fact that she could have asked him to do absolutely anything and he would have said 'yes'. Anything to get her to put her lips around his throbbing cock. *Anything*. Still looking back at him, she smiled again. She had him. He wasn't going anywhere. Careful not to knee him in the face she positioned herself so that her pussy hovered above Jacob's face. It was close enough to give him a full-on view but a little too far away for him to be able to get his mouth near it. 'Sit on my face,' he said again, as desperate to taste her juices as he was to feel her take him in her mouth. The words he spoke weren't a demand, more of a plea. She was in control here, just as she had been all night. He was merely a pawn in her game and soon to be - unknown to him - her latest victim. 'Please,' he begged louder this time, 'sit on my face. I want to taste you.' Harley wrapped her hand around the shaft of his cock and started to gently stroke up and down as she slowly lowered herself down to Jacob's face. He craned his neck up towards her cunt so as to get his tongue to it faster and - as soon as she was close enough - he gave her a lick, tasting what he thought to be her juices. *Lubricant gives the impression of wetness which, in turn, gives the impression of enjoyment.* Harley let out a sigh. It wasn't one of pleasure but it didn't matter. Jacob couldn't tell the difference as he craned his neck further, pushing his tongue into her slimy slit. Moans of pleasure, from both the feeling of her hand on his dick and the taste of her pussy on his tongue, purred from his throat as she too pretended to make the right noises. Her face told a different story though, one he would have seen had she not been sitting directly on his face blocking him from the room's one mirror which would have presented him the perfect view of it. Pain. It was happening. From inside her, definite movement. Jacob suddenly felt resistance against his tongue, as he continued fucking her pussy with it. He pulled out, confused. *Was something there?*

'If you're interested,' Harley said, 'I have a sister who can join us.' There was a sinister tone in her voice that went unnoticed by Jacob. He hadn't even heard her. He was more confused about what his tongue had felt up inside Harley's vagina. He lowered his head back down to the pillow to get a fuller view of her pussy. He screamed as - from between her lips - an adult-sized eyeball looked directly back at him. It blinked.

<u>#14</u>

BEFORE

<u>The Body.</u>

The room was cold. Sterile steel surfaces and not a spec of dirt anywhere to be seen. Rooms like this, Harley thought, were designed for function rather than style. She looked at the man across the room, who looked back over the top of his glasses.

“Are you ready?” he asked her, his voice echoing from the walls.

She wasn’t sure if she would ever be ready or if anything could ever make a person ready to do what she was about to do. Harley took a deep breath, looked the man in the eye and nodded. ‘Yes. I’m ready.’

The man turned to the recessed doors in the wall and opened one, then slid out the drawer, the body on it covered with a white sheet. Harley looked at the pathologist then at the sheet.

‘Just when you’re ready. This can be quite daunting.’ He said, giving her a well-practiced smile of compassion.

Harley stared at the sheet, her throat dry, the silence in the room maddening. She was sure she could hear her blood as it was pumped around her body. The pathologist was waiting patiently for her, slender hands folded in front of him. She nodded then stared at the sheet ready to see what was underneath it.

'Before I proceed,' the pathologist said, forcing her to take her eyes from the sheet. 'Did the police inform you of the injuries to the deceased?'

She nodded.

'I would suggest at this time that you prepare yourself. The identification process is never easy for the family members.'

Harley looked at him then at the sheet. 'Thank you. I'm prepared.'

The pathologist pulled back the sheet, folding it back to the upper breast-bone of the body on the table. Harley drew breath, the last hope that a mistake had been made banished. She couldn't breathe and for a moment thought she was going to pass out.

'Are you alright?' the mortuary assistant asked.

She nodded. 'Yes I'm fine, I'm....' She looked at the assistant then realised he was waiting for something. 'It's her. This is my sister.'

The mortuary assistant wrote something on his clipboard. 'Would you like a little time alone with the deceased?

She nodded, then as he was leaving spoke. 'She looks different. Her mouth seems...sunken.'

The mortuary assistant walked around to stand beside her and together they looked at the body. 'Her teeth were broken. Most of them missing.'

'How?'

She was beaten and many were lost that way. We also believe some were forcibly removed post mortem and kept as souvenirs.'

A wave of nausea swept over her and again she thought her legs were going to fail her.

'Are you sure you're alright?'

'Not really, I mean, I will be its just....we are *we were* twins. It's almost like looking at myself down there.'

'I understand how that can be upsetting. I'll give you some time alone. Just take as long as you need.'

Harley waited until he had left the room then looked down at her sister's body. 'Why did this have to happen?' she whispered. She looked at Cherrelle's body and realised all the things they would never do again. No more banter, no more joking about men or shopping trips on weekends. 'People say twins share a bond, a psychic connection that normal people don't have, but I don't... I mean I didn't feel anything. I didn't know where you were and I don't know if you could feel me but...does that mean we weren't as close as we thought? If we had that bond do you think I could have helped you?"

She let the question hang in the silence of the room. 'It's always been Cherrelle and Harley, now it will just be Harley. I don't think I'll get used to that for a long time. There were all these things. Things we wanted to do together and now we can't. It's so unfair.'

Harley wiped her eyes and tried to remember the last words the two of them had shared, but no matter how hard she tried, she couldn't recall.

'I don't know how you must have suffered. The police said he'd done awful things to you. You weren't the first and he's still out there. If there's any justice, any at all, he'll be caught and pay for dumping you in that field for the animals to eat. I...'

She stopped, sure the pathologist had come back into the room. She looked around, frowning as the door was still closed. She felt a knot in her stomach and looked down at the body on the table. 'Is that you? Are you here with me?' She looked down at the body on the table, expecting to see it move, to perhaps see her sister sit up and say it had all been a joke or a misunderstanding. The body, however, stayed as it was, grey skin, cuts and bruises standing out in stark clarity, the finger-shaped bruises on her neck. Harley, however, knew she wasn't alone. She could feel something in the room, an energy, a presence. A rash of goosebumps rippled across her arms as she looked at the dull polished steel drawers that, other than the one containing her sister were closed. The room was reflected back, a dull detail free reflection. She could see herself, her white shirt and jeans reflected well, her hair sitting on her shoulders. She could also see the mass behind her, the shifting undulating black tendrils which were sliding towards her from behind, melding together and forming shapes. Harley couldn't move. She was rooted to the spot, watching the formless thing approach her from behind. She could sense it there, an energy in the room akin to that of the air just before a thunderstorm, the taste of static, the sheer force of energy around her. If this was her sister, it was a different incarnation. The sister she had known was a sweet, kind person who loved life and was always looking to have a good time. The presence in the room felt different. She supposed it was understandable. The rage, the frustration. The anger at losing a young life at the hands of a monster, to a man who humiliated her and did vile things to her before dumping her naked in a field like a piece of forgotten furniture.

Yes.

She could understand that darkness. She could understand the fury and sense the thirst for vengeance. But it was still her sister, and she convinced herself it was all in her mind until she felt the hot breath on her neck and a brief hint of Cherrelle's favourite perfume.

Harley screamed, screamed and collapsed, her legs giving way. The pathologist ran into the room, trying to help her to her feet, telling her such shock was normal, and that grief was a natural part of the healing process. Harley didn't listen. She could only stare at the steel drawers. Her reflection was once again hers and hers alone, but she knew that her sister's presence, the thing so filled with fury and the thirst for vengeance was with her now and forever. Their bond was in life as it was in death, an unbreakable connection that she knew would be part of her forever. A quest for vengeance that she would undertake on behalf of her sister, no matter what the cost to herself.

#15

NOW

For My Sister.

The eyeball moved back inside Harley's pussy and the outer lips closed, hiding the horror. Jacob screamed again, still shocked by what he had seen, when the lips suddenly parted again revealing a mouth. It smiled at Jacob.

'Kiss me,' it said. It parted its lips and flicked its tongue up and down. Harley was laughing as Jacob squirmed beneath her body where she had him pinned.

'Get the fuck off me!' he screamed over and over again. They always screamed. The only comfort Harley took was that it never lasted for long. Her sister toyed with them for a while but her playful mood was quick to turn towards wanting vengeance for what had happened to her in that room; blaming all men for what happened. *All men are the same, all men deserve to die.*

'Don't be scared,' Harley said, 'it's just my sister. She always comes out to meet people like you.' Harley wrapped her hand around Jacob's dick and started squeezing as hard as she could in an effort to stop him from squirming beneath her. He wasn't a big man but she knew, if she didn't try and take control of him, he would end up throwing her off. And with no one pinning him down, it wouldn't be long before he started running. Not that it mattered. Her sister, Cherrelle, would still do what needed to be done. Once she has been seen, they never survive. It's just - if Harley can keep it contained to the one room - it ends up being *quieter* and less of a mess is made. Still, with his cock and balls in her hands, he wasn't going anywhere. 'You trying to tell me you don't want twins? I thought that was every guy's fantasy?' Harley laughed again. She sat up, pressing her full weight down on Jacob's face pussy-first. He flapped his arms beneath her, clearly panicking. Harley's laugh stopped. Something had snatched her attention away from what was happening. Her sister. Cherrelle. She was standing at the foot of the bed in the same ripped clothes she had been wearing when Harley identified the body in the morgue. Her face was pale. Her eyes sunken back and black in colour. In-human. Her long dark hair was greasy and matted, twisted and tangled. Harley's heart skipped a beat just as it always did when she saw her standing there. She both hated seeing her and loved it in equal measures. It was always a shock and she hated seeing her in this state - her loving sister - yet at least she got to see her. When other people lost someone they cared about, that was it. There was no seeing them again. At least Harley had this. 'I missed you,' she said. She always said this when she saw her. Cherrelle didn't respond. Harley didn't even know if she understood her. The way she craned her head to the side and looked at her, mouth slightly agape with a gravelly rasp coming from it, Harley at least knew she heard her. *Does she understand?* 'I got you another one,' Harley said. The same routine every year on the anniversary Cherrelle's life was taken from her, or at least - when Harley had to identify the body. *Couldn't bring her back but could help her get vengeance.* Harley suddenly screamed out as Jacob sunk his teeth into her cunt. Pinned between her thighs, he wasn't able to rip his head to the side - pulling the lips off in the process - but at least the sudden bolt of pain he'd issued was enough to get Harley to sit up, lifting her weight from him. That, in turn, was enough freedom for him. It allowed him the opportunity to throw her to the floor where she landed with a heavy thud. He sat up, wiping blood from his face, and saw - for the first time - Cherrelle standing there, staring right back at him with pure hatred in her eyes. She screamed at him, raising her hand towards him. Her fingers, twisted and broken, pointing as best as they could. *She sees him.*

'Please. Why are you doing this? Just stay back... I don't know what this is but... Just let me go home... Please...' His begging was pathetic.

Harley sat up from where she'd landed on the floor, hard. She laughed as she pulled herself up, using the bed as support. 'What do you want? Money? Is that it?' He knew it wasn't to do with money. He knew it was something much, much darker at hand. A man who didn't believe in the supernatural had changed his viewpoint in a split second at the sight of Cherrelle standing at the foot of the bed - her feet a couple of inches raised from the floor and her hair floating as though she herself was underwater. Even though he knew what she was, he didn't want to admit it to himself. He couldn't. 'Please let me go home...' Cherrelle slowly shook her head from side to side, her breathing hard and heavy - rasping.

'No one goes home.' Harley spoke in a matter of fact tone laced with a hint of sadness. Cherrelle screamed as she moved over the bed, horizontal in the air with her face now close to Jacobs. He screamed out as piss leaked from his flaccid dick, staining the white sheets on the hotel mattress yellow. 'No one gets to go home,' Harley said again.

A telephone, resting on the bedside cabinet, started to ring. Harley looked at it but ignored it's incessant rings. No need to answer it. She knew who it would be: a jumped-up receptionist calling up to check that everything was okay after another resident made a complaint about the noise. It wasn't a problem though. Cherrelle never let this moment drag on for longer than entirely necessary. By the time anyone came up - there would be nothing in the room but a fresh corpse.

'I don't understand why you're doing this!' Jacob shouted as he pulled his hands up to protect his face from Cherrelle as she continued to get closer. The foul stench of rotten breath making him want to gag.

She spoke in a whisper. An inhuman growl coming from the back of her throat with the word 'Vengeance' longer and more drawn out than it should have been.

'I haven't done anything to you! I haven't done anything to anyone!' Harley had heard it all before. All of the men protested their innocence moments before they died. The sentence unwittingly making up their final words. She turned away. She didn't like what followed.

Cherrelle who had moved so slow and steady, in single fluid and purposeful motions, suddenly lunged forward. Her hands wrapped around Jacob's shaking face. He fought to get her off, pulling at her hands as he screamed over and over again. Her grip got tighter around his head. His eyes bulged in their sockets, forced outward by the immense pressure. His skull cracked, fracturing in her superhuman grip. Beneath the skin the bone split in various directions, starting at the point of pressure. With her eyes shut tight and only the sound to tell her what was happening,

Harley tried to think of something else, *anything* else. She thought about running round the family garden, growing up, trying to capture butterflies on beautiful sunny days. She tried to think of shopping in town, with her sister, looking to spend money they had saved from various completed chores. She tried to think of staying up late, trying to scare each other with ghost stories... She tried to think of anything other than the suffering and pain and not because she didn't like thinking about what the victims were going through. She didn't like the torment because it always made her think about what her sister had gone through before she was murdered.

Jacob's scream changed in pitch. His eye balls popped from their sockets and hung down on the optic nerve, swinging there like a child's toy. Cherrelle moaned and twisted Jacob's head violently to the side. His neck cracked and his screaming stopped. The room was silent other than a heavy, authoritative knocking from out in the corridor.

The hotel manager called through, 'Sir? Sir can you open the door, please? Sir? Is everything okay in there?' His voice quietened as he spoke to someone else out in the corridor, 'Get it open...' There was fumbling beyond the door before a keycard was slid into the magnetic lock. The lock flashed green signifying it was unlocked and - a second later - the door was pushed open. The manager was in first. He stopped dead with security piling up behind him. All of them were open-mouthed and silent. Their eyes fixed on the corpse on the bed, its neck twisted and head facing the other direction. There was no one else in the room. 'Phone 999,' the manager mumbled, struggling with his words.

'What happened?' one of the security guards muttered as the second one leaned into the bathroom to see if there was anyone hiding in there. No one. The guest was definitely alone. 'How could he do this to himself?'

The manager yelled, 'I said phone 999!' The security guard pulled his mobile phone from his jacket as the manager scanned the room once more. 'How is this possible?' he asked.

#16

BEFORE

Vengeance.

It was a lie.

The idea that time healed and made grief more bearable was bullshit. Two months after the death of her sister and Harley was just as bitter and alone, the loss of her sibling leaving a huge gaping hole in her life. For a while, she lived on in hope that the man who had brutally raped and murdered Cherrelle would be brought to justice. She had put her faith in the system to help her, and in the end, it had failed. Not only had her sister's killer not been caught, he had killed twice more since, each time getting away without consequence. The truth was she was sick. Sick of living in hope, sick of the excuses given to her by the police, and sick of the void, the huge hole left in her life which was ripped from her when her sister was taken.

She sat in the club, drink untouched in front of her and watched the mass of humanity as they danced and gyrated, all of them trying to impress, to flirt or fuck. The music was loud, the room sweaty and hot. A few years ago in a different lifetime, she would have been down there on the dance floor doing the same. Flirting. Dancing. Fucking. Back when there was joy in her life back when there was a purpose other than revenge. Back before she started to see humanity for the twisted thing it really was beneath the smiles and insincerity.

Before she had decided to take things into her own hands.

She sipped her drink, watching a man try to chat up a woman, his hands gesticulating as he tried to impress, his words drowned out by the baseline. His target seemed unimpressed and soon walked away, lost in the writhing mass of bodies on the dance floor.

Yes.

Things had definitely changed and now she was taking things into her own hands. She got up and walked onto the dance floor, the world around her closing up and becoming a living breathing wall of flesh. She kept walking ignoring the people until she was on the opposite side of the room. The steps leading to the exit were to her left, and for a moment, she considered using them and forgetting this idea which she couldn't remember coming up with in the first place. Instead, she went into the bathroom, the volume of the music reduced to a dull rumble, the heat less in here. a group of girls in dresses too short and showing too much stood by the mirror touching up makeup and comparing notes on some of the men they had encountered that night. One was telling the other how she had been fingered in the corner by an ex who she thought she would probably take home that night. Her friend, perhaps sensing the car crash to come, was trying to talk her out of it. Harley went into one of the vacant cubicles and locked the door. She sat down, listening to the shrill voices of the girls at the mirrors. It was as she sat there, headache thundering that Harley realised she couldn't remember the last time she had slept. Sleep brought nightmares of her sister, but not as Harley remembered her. In her frequent nightmares, Cherrelle was a formless thing, a black mass of vengeance and anger, a creature seeking vengeance by proxy who would invariably ask Harley to help her. As always happened, Harley would wake screaming and clutching the sheets, sure her sister was there in the room with her until the nightmare faded. They were more than dreams, she was sure of that. They were terrifying and filled Harley with guilt that she could do nothing to help. And so she had stopped sleeping and had gone beyond exhaustion. She thought a few days without the dreams would help her break out of the cycle of depression she was in, but even that hadn't helped.

She had started to sense her sister when she was awake too. It was hard to explain how she knew her sister was there. It was a sense, an uncomfortable feeling of cold and oppression surrounding her. Ideas that weren't hers started to form in her head. Ideas of how to best avenge the brutal and unfair death of her sister. The police couldn't help. That much as obvious. It was down to her to avenge what happened and today was the day it would begin.

She waited until the mirror girls left the room before she came out of the stall. The bathroom was now empty, but she knew it wouldn't stay that way for long. The door had a lock, and she walked to it and slid it into place, not wanting to be disturbed. She then went to the mirror and looked at herself. Her skin was pale and waxy, eyes ringed from lack of sleep. Her hair had taken on a dull and listless look and she convinced herself she didn't care until she saw her reflection crying and realised she did care. She cared about justice. She cared about a god she no longer believed in and how he could allow her sister to die in such an awful manner. She cared about revenge against man. A species who thought with its genitals rather than its brain. She set her bag down by the sink and took out the knife and set it on the counter in front of her.

'I don't know if I can do this, Sis.' She whispered to her reflection. 'I don't think I'm strong enough.' She waited, knowing what was coming. Unlike the first time in the morgue, Harley didn't scream as the thing started to form behind her reflection. She knew if she turned around there would be nothing there. She watched as it formed, the undulating black mass of tendrils a shapeless entity that pulsed around her. She didn't see her sister, not as a physical form, but she *felt* her. Her arms flashed with goosebumps. She stared at the mass behind her and knew what she had to do.

'We'll get your revenge.' She muttered. 'We'll do it together.'

She picked up the knife and pulled it across her throat, her reflection lost in a claret spray. She felt herself fading, finally able to rest finally free of the life she had grown to hate. Finally free to get her revenge.

*****

'What do you think, Martin?'

Andrews looked at the bloody thing strewn across the bed that used to be a man, then at Patterson who was looking at him, the old buzzard expecting him to have some grand revelation. "I don't know yet.' Andrews replied, crouching by the body and looking into the dead man's eyes.

'The same killer?" Patterson asked as forensics took photos around them.

'Definitely. Same setup. Same result. Where did you find the rest of him?' Andrews said, nodding at the gaping hole where the man's genitals used to be.

'In the bathroom sink.' Patterson said. 'It looked all mangled and chewed up like the others.'

Andrews stood, frowning at the scene trying to remember a time when he cared about the people involved rather than getting a result. 'Let me guess. No witnesses.'

Patterson shook his head. 'Like with the others. The guy checked in alone. Nobody saw anyone come or go. We're checking CCTV now but-'

'You won't find anything.' Andrews said. Walking to the window and looking out across the street. 'This makes no sense.'

'Does it ever?' Patterson grumbled, joining him at the window.

'No, I mean the setup this whole thing.'

'What are you thinking, Martin?'

Andrews looked around the room, a frown on his brow, and then back to the window. 'We know our killer likes to bring their victims to cheap hotels, right?'

'We do.' Patterson agreed.

‘Put yourself in the killer’s shoes for a second. Look over there’ Andrews nodded across the street. ‘This room is overlooked from directly across the street by at least three windows.’ plus the walls are paper thin. I don’t understand why they would take the risk here.’

‘This city is full of crazy people, Martin. It’s getting worse.’

‘Tell me about it. I’m drowning in work.’

‘I actually wanted to talk to you about that. Next week we have a new kid coming in from the academy.’

Andrews sighed, knowing what was coming. ‘Who am I babysitting?’

‘It’s not like that, Martin. This kid is good. Top of his class. Perkins is his name. Young and full of ideas.’

‘You say that like I’m old and ready for retirement.’ Andrews grumbled.

‘You know I don’t mean it like that. All I’m saying is it will take the pressure off you a bit. Share the workload. I’ve heard...I’ve heard you and Lucy are having a few issues. This job isn’t kind to marriages, Martin.’

Andrews hid his irritation at the probing into his private life. ‘Lucy and I are fine. Actually, we just found out she’s pregnant last week.’

Patterson grinned, genuinely happy. ‘That’s wonderful news, Martin. Congratulations.’

Andrews didn't return the smile. 'Is it? In this world today where stuff like this happens, do I really want to bring a kid into it?" Patterson frowned and was about to speak before Andrews cut him off, not wanting to get into a conversation about his wife. 'Anyway, enough about that. This new guy you're bringing in, Perkins. Can't you put him with Wyatt or something? You know I prefer to work on my own.'

'Wyatt is with Richards. You need an extra set of hands.'

'Fine,' Andrews snapped, knowing it was pointless to argue. 'You're the boss.'

'So this murder. What are we thinking?'

Andrews looked around the room taking in the information and trying to reconstruct what had happened. 'Whoever is doing this is good. We know that by the lack of evidence. Nothing left at any crime scene. Not even a hair or fibre. That alone is unusual. Then there is the fact that nobody ever actually sees the killer. The victims all check in alone to the hotels in question and seemingly die that way. The one last month in the park. A public place, a place where anyone could have discovered them at any time and yet our killer didn't care.'

'They made a mess of that one too,' Perkins said.

'Exactly. If you're going to cut someone's balls off and shove them down their own throat, you want privacy.'

'So our killer is reckless. Surely that's a good sign.'

Andrews shook his head. 'No, because the rest of it makes no sense. On one hand they are careful in not getting seen with the victim and somehow escaping the same way. I mean, just look at this room. Blood everywhere. How does our killer get out without getting bloody clothes?'

'So we're looking for someone careful and meticulous.'

'Are we?' Andrews said, nodding again out of the window. 'Then how do we explain the reckless murder locations. Overlooked rooms, public places. To inflict the level of violence that this killer perpetrates is next level. Someone so careful would want seclusion. Privacy. It makes no sense at all.'

'Somebody must know something.' Patterson grunted.

'Tell me about it. I've never known a case be so cold as far as leads go. This is the sixth one and not a shred of evidence. I hate to say it, but I'm stumped. I genuinely have no idea where we go from here.'

Patterson stared out of the window, and Andrews realised just how old he was looking. 'I'll tell you one thing, Martin. With the level of violence, with the fury of how they do this....It's not going to end anytime soon. You know that, don't you?'

Andrews nodded and said nothing. He was more than aware. Even the most careful killer left evidence behind no matter how hard they tried. He had convicted a rapist once on the evidence of a single fibre from a jacket he was wearing which had attached itself to his victim's skin. No evidence at all was beyond unusual. It was impossible. All they could do now was wait for the killer to strike again and hope they made a mistake.

NOW

Detective Patterson stepped into the hotel room, followed by his partner Reeves. The hotel manager was with them, showing them the crime scene he'd burst in on.

'We checked the CCTV footage,' the manager started to explain.

Patterson cut him off, 'Let me guess - you saw no one come or go from the room?'

'We have him checking in, we have him coming to the room... We have a few people walking down the corridor. We even have the next room sticking their head into the corridor - looking in the direction of this room.

They must have tried to see if they could see what was happening before they phoned down to reception.' He shook his head. 'What we don't have is anyone else going in or coming out of the room.'

'You said someone phoned down to the reception?'

'Yes. The room next door. They phoned down to complain about the noise. They said they heard a man screaming. We phoned up to this room to see if we could find out what was happening - presumed it could have been a television on too loud. We don't normally have guests shouting and screaming in the rooms so it would have made sense. When they didn't answer we came up. It was myself and the security guards. We knocked on the door, could hear him screaming. When no one replied, we used one of our keys to get in.'

'And you found him like this.'

'Yes.'

Patterson looked to Reeves. Neither man needed to tell the other one that they were dealing with another victim of an unsolved case going back years now. Same date, same mysterious circumstances and always male victims. And - as always...

'No one saw anything?' Patterson confirmed.

'Nothing.'

... No witnesses.

'I've worked in other hotels and I've seen guests die for various reasons... Had one man have a heart attack during a vigorous session with a call girl he booked but... Damned if I have ever seen anything like this. What do you think? Suicide?' The manager looked back to the corpse. He realised suicide was probably not the cause of death but - with no people coming or going from the room, what else could it have been?

Patterson walked him from the room with Reeves following close behind, leading the manager away from the crime scene before it got contaminated. He always knew there would be no evidence in the room - nothing to help solve the case - but, even so, it didn't mean they wouldn't try and find something of use. 'We're going to have to ask that no one comes up here. Forensics will be here shortly and we will try and see what we can find out for you and - of course - we're going to need a list of the other guests on this floor so we can arrange to interview them...'

'Interview the other guests? Is that entirely necessary?'

'Someone might have seen something.' Patterson knew no one had seen anything. More than that, he knew this was a case that was never going to be solved. If it was solvable, his old partner Detective Martin Andrews would have solved it. He was one of the best the force had... Once upon a time, before what happened to his wife and child. So many years ago. A thought which highlighted how long *this* crime had been going on for. Another year, another victim and another wad of paperwork for the file. Patterson sighed. He wasn't normally a defeatist but he knew the rest of the day would be pointless police work but it didn't mean he could get away with not doing it. Procedure. Even Reeves, his new partner fresh from graduation, knew of the case and the chances of it ever being solved.

'I'll get you the names,' the manager said.

'And we need the media to be kept away. Unless you want your hotel shut whilst we investigate, I'd suggest you get security on the doors and if anyone asks why the police presence - you don't give them any answers. Understood?' Patterson's words were strict and the manager took them seriously. He nodded. 'Good.'

'I'll be back soon with the names,' the manager said as he headed off towards the elevators.

'Thank you.'

Patterson pulled the bedroom door closed just in case anyone walked past and looked in. Reeves didn't say anything. He didn't ask if Patterson had any hunches, he just stood there - unsure of what to do. He had heard of this case because it was legend around the station but this was the first time he had been involved in it directly. Last year, when the murderer last struck, he was still finishing his exams and now… Now he was responsible for helping to crack the uncrackable.

'Why only once a year?' Reeves asked eventually. He knew Patterson couldn't give an accurate answer. Only the killer knew why they did it once a year but, he figured, Patterson could at least give his best hunch.

Patterson shrugged. 'Anniversary of some relevance I'd hazard a guess.' He sighed and turned to Reeves. 'We might just have to come to the terms with the fact we may never know.'

Reeves recalled the look of the victim. He recalled the way the eyes hung from their sockets. He shuddered. 'Someone who does that to another human being though… What do they do for the rest of the year? How can they do *this* to someone and then carry on their lives as though nothing has happened?'

'Who knows what goes through the mind of a murderer?' Patterson sighed again. Maybe Andrews had it right? Maybe it was best to just retire? So much evil in the world, he had said, that you'd never get rid of it all. A never ending battle. Maybe he was right? He sighed again. It was going to be a long day made more frustrating given he knew the outcome was going to be the same, just as it had been every other year this killer had struck.

'You think they just sit there - waiting?'

Patterson shrugged. He had had enough of talking now. He would have preferred it if Reeves just shut up yet he didn't have the heart to tell him to do so. Patterson was tired. 'Maybe,' he agreed.

#17

JUST UNDER A YEAR LATER

Waiting.

The nightclub was practically empty. Only cleaners milled around, mopping up sticky spillages from the night before. The well-played dance music - hits from past and present - had been replaced with classics from the 80s. The music of choice for the cleaners who liked to sing along as they worked.

Half eleven in the morning. The shift was coming to an end and the bar was gleaming, ready for another night of mess and mayhem. The dance-floor had also been cleaned, along with the carpets around the building - not that the latter came up perfectly. They were well-worn with people traipsing over them in their dirty shoes and dropping drinks on them. They wouldn't be replaced though. Management didn't deem it necessary considering - when the main lights were off and club lights shining - you couldn't really notice anything on the floor. Still, all was clean with the exception of the one room no one liked doing and not for the obvious reasons. The ladies' bathroom.

'It's your turn,' Heidi said to Alex as she put her mop up against the wall. She pointed towards the bathroom with a nod of her head. There'd be smears on the mirror, litter on the floor, splash-marks around the sink, toilet paper on the floor, stains in the bowl and sometimes used condoms dropped in cubicles too - none of which was a problem for any of the cleaners. It was an unpleasant part of their job but they knew there was little point in worrying about it, or moaning. The sooner they started clearing it away, the sooner it was done. And - besides - they had protective gear to wear to stop any of the mess getting on their skin or clothes.

'I did it yesterday,' Alex moaned.

'No, you didn't. I did. It was supposed to be you doing it yesterday but you said you had to leave early. I ended up doing it for you...'

'Please - I don't...'

'No. It's not my turn. You're doing it.'

Alex sighed heavily. She didn't want to do it but she could tell by Heidi's voice and facial expression that she wasn't going to get out of it today. Especially after her stunt yesterday - having to leave early. A lie to get out of having to go in the bathroom. 'You'll come in with me?' Heidi shook her head. 'At least wait here, yeah?'

'Fine. Just hurry up.' Heidi didn't need to tell Alex to hurry up. It would be the fastest Alex had ever worked. No one hung around in there.

Alex turned to the door, mop in hand, and slowly approached. Whenever there was a slight pause in the music's loud beat, or the vocals went quiet, they could hear the weeping from beyond the door. The lonely cries of a heartbroken woman which stopped the moment any of them stepped into the room. Despite the room going silent, the cleaners knew they weren't alone. Not in that room. And they weren't either. It wasn't a figment of their imagination. The cries they thought they heard - they were true. They came from the last cubicle in the room where Harley sat - unseen - on the toilet seat, waiting for the anniversary to come around so that she could once again leave. Her tears weren't the only ones haunting a room though. A few miles away there was a little room... Huddled in the corner of which, a young lady cried for her freedom, cried for her vengeance. She cried for the life stolen from her. Cherrelle screamed out.

With thanks to

Grant Oxford

Betty Lynn

Joan MacLeod

Lauriette Hutzler

Jarod Barbee

Stacy Latini

Sophie Hall

Scott Hunter

Hayley Marcham

Leah Cruz

Kelly Rickard

Barry Skelhorn

Alicia Green

Jennifer Burg Pelfrey

Chad Ferguson

Nancy Loudin

Your continued support means the world to me.

Thank you.

Made in the USA
Las Vegas, NV
18 June 2021

25009300R00056